IT'S OKAY TO TRUST FRIENDS, RIGHT?

Nichelle groaned. "So guess what," she said, changing the subject with her friends. "Mr. Toussaint stopped me on the way out, and he asked me to write an extra article for the *Generation Beat*. Just a thousand words or so. Like I have time."

"Sure you do," grinned Ana. "Dinnertime. You don't have to eat, right?"

"Maybe," said Barbie, "you could do an article on . . . well, you know. The thing we're interested in." Nichelle knew that Barbie wouldn't let their secret slip, even to their best friends.

But of course, saying "well, you know" in front of their friends was like yelling "Fire!" in a crowded theater. Suddenly, four sets of eyes were totally riveted on Nichelle and Barbie.

"What?" said Ana. "What's 'well, you know'?"

"Come on," said Chelsie, "give."

Nichelle thought about it for a minute, and then she decided she could let their friends in on the secret. They knew when to keep their mouths shut.

"Okay," she said to them, "but you have to sit on this. No blabbing. It's important."

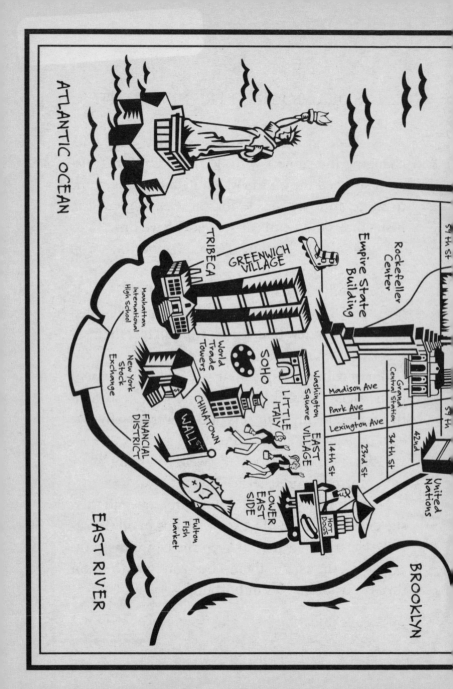

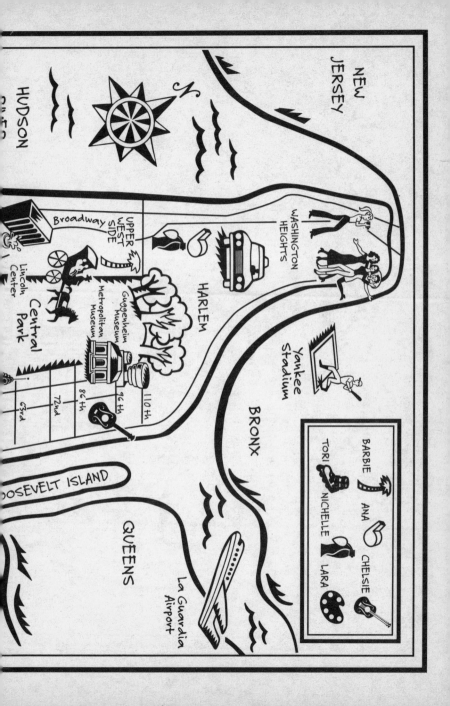

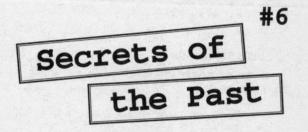

GENERATI*N GIRL

#6

Secrets of
the Past

By Melanie Stewart

A GOLD KEY PAPERBACK
Golden Books Publishing Company, Inc.
New York

A GOLD KEY Paperback Original

Golden Books Publishing Company, Inc.
888 Seventh Avenue
New York, NY 10106

Cover photography by Graham Kuhn

Interior art by Amy Bryant

0-307-23455-X

First Gold Key paperback printing August 1999

10   9   8   7   6   5   4   3   2   1

Printed in the U.S.A.

GENERATI✳N GIRL

Secrets of
the Past

Chapter 1

Trouble in City Hall

Nichelle Watson fell into the easy chair in the corner of her mother's large office and dropped her silver backpack onto the floor. She secured her long curly hair up onto the top of her head with a band, stretched out her slim chestnut-colored legs, and closed her eyes. It had been one of those not-enough hours, running-to-catch-up kind of days, and it felt good to be here in this quiet room deep inside City Hall.

Nichelle wondered what was keeping her mother. She was probably in a meeting with the mayor. Mrs. Watson had been working for the mayor of New York City for as long as Nichelle could remember, and now that she was a student at Manhattan International High School it was great. Most afternoons, when the final bell rang and she said goodbye to her friends, Nichelle walked over to City Hall to meet her mother. When Mrs. Watson was ready, they rode the subway home to Harlem together. It was nice. It gave them a chance to talk before her father, who was head of pediatrics at Harlem Hospital, came home from work, and before her older brother, Shawn, burst through the front door, and the evening madness began.

Those subway rides had brought them even closer together than they already were. They talked about everything under the sun — work, school, people, life. Nichelle learned that her mother's favorite color as a teenager had been purple, just as it was now Nichelle's. She shared her latest crush with her mother, which Nichelle had to admit changed practically every day. One of the best things about their ride home every evening was that Nichelle learned more about her mother's upbringing in Philadelphia. It was cool to hear about the high society world that had been a part of her parent's early life.

Most of all, Nichelle loved listening to her

mother talk about her job. "New York's finest historical preservationist," she called herself, jokingly. But Nichelle knew it wasn't a joke. Her mother was good at her work, and she really cared about preserving New York City's past. It wasn't easy; the job came with a different headache every day, as she tried to balance the needs of architects, real estate developers, and the city's amazing past. "Once it's gone," she always said, "it's gone." She told Nichelle about New York's famed Penn Station, one of the most majestic train stations in the country, and how it had fallen to the wrecking ball and was now lying in great, sad chunks at the bottom of the wetlands in New Jersey.

"To top it off," she'd told Nichelle with a shake of the head and a sad smile, "the government is thinking about replacing it. It's going to cost billions."

Now, in the easy chair, Nichelle opened her eyes and glanced at her oversized silver watch. She stood up and began to pace. She was anxious to get home. Where was her mother? Nichelle had an English paper due the next day, and she still had a lot of work left on it because of a catalog-modeling job she'd been doing for the past few days.

Nichelle walked over to the door and looked out

at the wide, well-lit hallway. It was another busy day at City Hall. As usual, the corridor was bustling, but there was no sign of her mother.

Nichelle spotted a tall, regal-looking woman in a stylish red business suit coming her way. Her mother was wearing the long earrings that Nichelle had given her for her birthday. They were made of tiny wooden beads, and set off her new short haircut perfectly. Nichelle thought she looked beautiful. Beautiful, but upset. Nichelle recognized by the way her mother walked that something was bothering her.

Mrs. Watson didn't notice Nichelle standing in the doorway. She was deep in conversation with a man that Nichelle recognized. His name was Mr. Evans, and he was one of the mayor's top advisors.

They stopped now, near the open door where Nichelle was standing. Mrs. Watson's back was to her daughter.

Uh-oh, Nichelle thought. *Something wicked's going on here.*

"I don't want you to mention this to anyone!" Mr. Evans was saying in a firm, controlled voice. "Not anyone! Do you understand? The mayor doesn't want a lot of publicity about this!"

4

Secrets of the Past

Mrs. Watson's body tightened as she stood facing Mr. Evans in silence. Nichelle slipped behind the door. She was almost sure that Mr. Evans hadn't seen her.

"That building can wait!" her mother said angrily, in a voice that was just a little too loud. "Curtis doesn't have to put his building up immediately. He has buildings all over Manhattan, so why can't he wait until we've done a site survey? No one knows for sure how big that burial ground is! It's not often that a building gets torn down and we get a chance to see what was under it before another one goes up. I'm not talking about stopping his construction, just putting it off by a few weeks."

Nichelle was beginning to understand. Her mother had been telling her about the African Burial Ground in lower Manhattan for a long time. Mrs. Watson had explained to her that New York had been one of the largest centers of slavery in the North. Nichelle could never get over the fact that there had been slaves right here in Manhattan for about two hundred years, starting in the early 1600s!

"The burial ground was where the slaves had

been buried by their friends and families," she had told Nichelle. "As the years passed, buildings were erected on it, and it was forgotten. Then, just a few years ago, it was rediscovered when they were excavating for a new building."

Her mother was very excited about the artifacts that archaeologists were discovering down there.

This Curtis guy must be getting ready to build another office building on or near the sacred site, Nichelle thought.

"It's about money!" Mrs. Watson was saying to Evans. "Everything's always about money! The money that Curtis contributed to the mayor's campaign, and that of every other politician in New York! The money that he'll make if his building goes up before we can examine his site."

"And the money you'll lose if you get fired over this!" Evans interrupted angrily.

"Are you threatening to fire me if I take this to the press?" Mrs. Watson sounded incredulous. "I know the mayor wouldn't put up with this if he knew."

"I'm threatening to fire you if you go to the press or anyone else. I'm even threatening to fire you if you go over my head to the mayor. Curtis is my responsibility! And his building is going up — soon!"

Nichelle heard Evans stomp away into the depths of City Hall. As her mother turned to the doorway, Nichelle raced back to the easy chair, fell into it, and closed her eyes again. If her mother knew that she had overheard this conversation, it would have caused her even more worry.

Mrs. Watson came in, closed the door, and took a deep breath. Nichelle could tell from the sound of that sigh that she was still angry. Nichelle and her mother were alike in many ways, and this was one of them. They did not like to show that they were angry. They weren't the kind of people who stomped around and shouted. They sighed and held it in.

At first Mrs. Watson didn't notice her daughter in the corner, pretending to be asleep, and when she finally did, she didn't mention the conversation. She just shook her head, shrugged, and yanked her coat from the hook next to the door.

"Hi Nikki," she sighed as she slid into her coat. "Let's go. I'm tired."

The evening passed without any mention of the incident, but Nichelle couldn't stop thinking about it. She wished that she hadn't heard it; eavesdropping was something that she would never do on purpose. Privacy mattered to Mrs. Watson, as it did to Nichelle, and they respected each other's space. She could tell that her mother was preoccupied, and Nichelle hated to see her mother upset, but if the conversation was none of her business, then she knew she shouldn't talk about it.

But Nichelle couldn't stop thinking about the African Burial Ground.

She was thinking about it as she settled down at the dinner table between her older brother, Shawn, and her father.

"You home for the night, Dad?" Shawn asked, as he took a large spoonful of mashed potatoes from the bowl that his mother had passed him.

"I'm afraid not," Dr. Watson said. "I have to go back to the hospital."

Nichelle thought that he sounded tired, too. Sometimes she worried that her parents worked too hard, and she wished that they could all spend more time together. But her father was a dedicated doctor. Deep down, she knew he wanted to spend more time with the family, too.

Dr. Watson patted his gray hair and adjusted his glasses. His gentle eyes looked weary.

"Sunday," he said. "Let's try and spend the whole day together on Sunday. Are you free, Shawn?"

"Sure," Shawn said, taking his third piece of chicken from the large blue plate in the middle of the table. "I'd like that. It's a date."

"How about you, Nichelle?" Dr. Watson asked. "No photo shoots?"

Nichelle knew that her father was a little worried about her growing love for modeling. She knew he would like her to concentrate on math and science, and that he had dreams of her becoming a doctor or a scientist. He came from a long line of doctors in the Watson family. But she knew that he respected her no matter what she did.

"No photo shoots on Sunday, Dad. So yes, I'm free. What should we do?"

There were so many things to choose from in New York City.

"How about an art exhibit?" Nichelle's mother suggested. The thought of a Sunday together with the whole family seemed to perk her up.

"I haven't been to a play in far too long," Dr.

Watson said. "Maybe we should try and get tick-
ets."

They tossed around options for several minutes,
until Nichelle came up with the one idea that
seemed to please everyone.

"Let's stay home," she said. "We never stay home.
We have the very best house in New York, and
nobody's ever in it."

She was right, of course. They had spent so
much time fixing up their beautiful, historic
brownstone in Hamilton Heights, one of the most
gracious neighborhoods in the entire city, just
north of City College. Down the street was the
house Alexander Hamilton had built for himself in
the 1700s. The neighborhood's streets were lined
with lovely brownstones and big trees, and each
house seemed to have a character all its own. The
Watsons' house had a huge mahogany front door,
complete with a heavy knocker in the shape of a
lion's head.

After years of work, the house was finally just
perfect. And now it seemed everyone was too busy
to appreciate all the special things about it: the
exposed brick wall in the kitchen, the herb garden

outside the back window, the fireplaces that they didn't use often enough.

"So let's stay home and light a fire and play Monopoly and Scrabble," she said. "How about that? We can ask M'dear to come over. She'd like that."

M'dear was Nichelle's grandmother, her father's mother, and everyone loved having her around. She was important to the whole family, but she was especially important to Nichelle. M'dear had helped to raise Nichelle and Shawn, and now that Nichelle was modeling, she accompanied her granddaughter to every photo shoot. By law, a model under the age of sixteen needed a guardian, and M'dear was Nichelle's. She enjoyed going along and watching.

M'dear lived about twenty blocks away, over by Columbia University. Nichelle's parents had been trying to persuade her to move into the brown-stone, but M'dear refused to consider it.

"I need my own place," M'dear had been saying ever since Nichelle could remember. "And so do you."

"A Sunday at home," Dr. Watson sighed. "That

sounds perfect. I promise that I will make arrangements not to be disturbed on Sunday if it's humanly possible. And Shawn, no basketball, okay?"

"Okay," Shawn laughed. "I promise not to touch a basketball for the entire day."

"I'll call M'dear tonight," Nichelle said. "I have to talk to her about the next shoot anyway."

"Give her my love," Dr. Watson said as he pushed back his chair. "In the meantime, it's back to the hospital. How's math coming, Nichelle, as if I didn't know?"

Nichelle always got A's in math. She was an honor roll student, good at everything, but math was her best subject.

After dinner, Nichelle insisted on doing the dishes alone. Shawn had basketball practice, and she wanted her mother to relax. Then she finished her English paper and was in bed by ten-thirty, wearing her favorite purple nightshirt. But before she turned out the lamp, she had one last thing to do. She snuggled down into her four pillows, arranged her little wooden writing board on her knees, and opened her packet of lavender stationery. She had a letter to write, one that was long overdue.

Dear Niecy,

I'm sorry it's been soooooo long since I wrote you. It's not that I haven't been thinking about my favorite cousin. It's just that I've been so busy, it's not even funny!

You know I started at a brand-new high school in September, right? I'm a sophomore like you, but everybody in the school is starting fresh because the school wasn't even there last year. It's a totally great place. Even though it's huge, they really care about every single student. And it has all kinds of stuff like new computers and art rooms and labs. There are a million kinds of kids there, and at first I was scared I wouldn't find any friends, but then things got way better. Now I have five of the best friends on earth: Barbie Roberts, Ana Suarez, Tori Burns, Chelsie Peterson, and Lara Morelli-Strauss. They're all different from me and each other, but maybe that's why it works.

Outside of school, my modeling career is starting to

take off. I can't believe it but it's true. It's really hard work, but it's so cool being a real model!

How are things in New Orleans? I miss all you guys so much! Everybody in my family's good, but I think my mom has the hardest job in New York. Shawn just grew past the six-feet mark. I can't beat him up any more.

Write me a letter! C'mon, I know you forgive me.

XOXOXO,
your best cuz, Nichelle

Chapter 2

Nichelle Chooses a Partner

Nichelle was thinking about the African Burial Ground as she slid into her seat in Mr. Budge's history class the next morning. Barbie was already there in the next seat, waiting for her. Nichelle was glad that she was in Barbie's history class now.

"There's been a mistake," Mr. Budge had explained to Nichelle a few days earlier. "The computer seems to have assigned too many students to my seventh period class. I'm afraid we'll have to move you to first period!"

Nichelle had been ecstatic. Her afternoon modeling assignments were beginning to pile up, and

15

now she could leave school by two o'clock, immediately after sixth period.

She wanted to talk to Barbie about the conversation she'd overheard about the African Burial Ground, but she wasn't sure if she should. Would it be a betrayal of her mother? She knew that Barbie would be fascinated. Barbie loved searching for hidden secrets. And at that very moment, Barbie's parents were digging for clues to the past somewhere on the other side of the world. While they were gone, Barbie was staying with a family on the Upper West Side of Manhattan and attending International High as an "exchange student." Maybe she was an exchange student from sunny Malibu, California, but she was an exchange student just the same.

"Have you ever heard of the African Burial Ground over by City Hall?" Nichelle whispered. Mr. Budge was straightening his papers in the front of the room, getting ready to start the class. The papers already seemed neat enough to Nichelle, but he kept shuffling them until they were in an absolutely perfect pile.

Mr. Budge was a perfectionist. But he was even more notorious for his penchant for personal cleanliness. He could spend an entire class worrying the tiniest thread on his sleeve or his collar.

Barbie shook her head.

Nichelle was just about to tell Barbie of the conversation that she had overheard, swearing her to secrecy, when Mr. Budge cleared his throat.

"You will recall that we were discussing the Civil War," he began, in a droning flat voice that put everyone to sleep. "I think that we were up to 1862. Before we go forward, does anyone have any questions on what we covered yesterday?"

Nichelle raised her hand, and Mr. Budge nodded.

"I have a question," she announced. "But it's not exactly about yesterday's class."

Mr. Budge grimaced, unhappy about being thrown off track. History was the love of Mr. Budge's life. He loved discussing battles and dates and all the little details that went into making his country great. And sometimes he got so carried away that he found interruptions painful.

"I have a question about slavery," Nichelle explained. "We've been learning about how the Civil War was mostly about freeing slaves in the South. Northerners wanted the slaves free, and

Southerners needed them to work their planta-
tions."

Mr. Budge nodded politely in agreement with
Nichelle.

She took a breath. "Mr. Budge," she continued,
"we've been reading all about slavery in the South.
But there is no mention at all in this textbook of
slavery in the North. Why don't we read about the
slavery right here? For instance, why doesn't it say
anything about that African Burial Ground down
by City Hall? How big was it?"

Mr. Budge didn't say anything for at least a
minute. He was thinking, and that often took a
long time.

"Well, Ms. Watson," he said at last, "I think the
thing for you to do is to find yourself a partner and
put together an extra-credit report. I think your
questions are quite interesting. And I for one will
be more than interested in what you uncover."

Nichelle nodded. "Okay," she said. "I'll look for a
partner."

Barbie leaned toward Nichelle. "Choose me!" she
pleaded in a whisper. "I'm desperate for extra-
credit! I need all the help I can get in history!"

Nichelle smiled. She could never quite understand

why Barbie had more problems with history than her other subjects, but everybody had a weakness, it seemed. Her brother Shawn, who took after their mother in his love of history, was tutoring Barbie in his favorite subject. History interested Nichelle, but it was not her greatest love. She was more interested in science and math. But what she adored was modeling.

Sometimes she wondered if she would be a model forever. Probably not. Most likely she'd go to college and choose the perfect career, whatever that meant. But right now, she was having a blast.

Mr. Budge had now turned to the blackboard and started writing a list of battles that took place during 1862.

Barbie leaned toward Nichelle again. "Choose me, okay?"

Nichelle smiled at Barbie. She opened her notebook and wrote a huge "Let's work on it together!" on a blank page. It would be great doing an extra-credit project with Barbie. She was a good reporter, and she was an expert at camera work. Barbie's video camera work had made their projects better. Working with Barbie would be awesome!

Barbie opened her notebook to a blank page and

wrote the words "Tell me more about the African Burial Ground!" in red ink.

"I need to learn a lot more about it," Nichelle wrote back. "Let's log onto the Internet tonight and see what we can come up with."

"Excellent!" Barbie whispered, a bit too loudly. "This should be fun!"

"Shhh," said Patty Weir, who sat behind Nichelle.

Near the end of the class, Mr. Budge described how the Battle of Gettysburg had caused President Lincoln to write his world-famous Gettysburg Address. ". . . [A]nd that government of the people, by the people, for the people shall not perish from the earth," Lincoln had said.

Those were good words, Nichelle thought.

Chapter 3

It Never Snows in July—Or Does It?

When history class was over, Barbie and Nichelle walked out of the room together. They were both excited about the burial ground project and couldn't wait till that evening to get started.

But as excited as Nichelle was about that, she was even more excited about her big photo shoot. She thought about it all day.

Nichelle had never worked for *Teen Style* before, and the whole idea of it was making her a little nervous. Up until now, her modeling career had consisted of small jobs, like catalogs or local newspaper ads.

But this was different. This was a national magazine!

"Hats," they had said. "You'll be modeling spring
hats for the shoot."

M'dear was going to meet her there. M'dear
would like that. She loved going to photo shoots
with her granddaughter, and Nichelle liked having
her. Nichelle knew from the pictures that were all
over the house that M'dear had been a great beauty
when she was younger. She still looked terrific.

Nichelle wondered what they were going to do
about the early November snow. Spring hats meant
that the shoot was for a spring issue of the magazine, which meant that the pictures would have to
show a spring scene. She couldn't wait to find out
what they were going to do about all that white
stuff on the grass.

Sitting in the music appreciation room waiting
for her third-period class to start, Nichelle pushed
the tiny button on the side of her watch and smiled
as the light blinked on and off, on and off. She
loved the great big watch. Her father had given it to
her five years ago on her tenth birthday, when she
had first said she wanted to be a model.

"Now that you'll be modeling, you'll never miss

an appointment," he had said. "All you have to do is push the button and it will light up. And it's waterproof, so you'll know what time it is even if you're ten feet underwater."

Nichelle knew that he'd been a little reluctant to see her enter the world of modeling, but she also understood that this had been his way of telling her that he supported her, no matter what she chose to do.

She checked the tiny perfume bottle charm that she always wore around her neck and smiled. Her other grandmother, her mother's mother, had given her that charm three years ago, just before she died, and filled it with her favorite fragrance, Tea Rose.

"When I was a little girl," her grandmother had told her, "my mother wore this perfume. I love the smell of it and have always worn it. Now you can wear it, too."

It made Nichelle feel special to have something to help her remember her grandmother. Whenever she smelled the perfume, she thought of wonderful hugs and family stories. Nowadays, Nichelle never took the charm off except to refill it.

The rest of the school day flew by, and at last,

sixth period was over. The huge school door slammed behind her, as she stopped and glanced at her watch. She had plenty of time if the train didn't get stuck, or a blizzard stranded her, or some massive traffic jam stopped her in her tracks. She knew she was worrying too much, but she did not want to be late for this shoot!

It was a glorious day! The sun was shining bright in the sky, warming her face and melting the snow. It could have been a summer sun, and in an hour or so it would be, when the lights were set up and everyone pretended that it was April.

Nichelle flew down the school steps and raced toward the subway. The subway platform was crowded with International High students carrying their books and chatting with their friends. At least ten juniors and seniors said "Hi," which surprised her. She was always amazed when the older kids greeted her, even though Barbie and Tori kept telling her that she was one of the more popular girls in the school.

"That's ridiculous!" she would protest. "I'm only a sophomore!"

But there it was. Everybody was greeting her.

Maybe it was because of her high visibility in the student government.

Nichelle smiled, said hi, and waved back, but she didn't stop to talk. She was too excited to do anything but peer into the dark tunnel to see if the train was coming. When it finally screeched to a stop, she pushed inside, grabbed a pole, and hung on. She hated being jostled and shoved around. So hanging onto a pole was the best insurance. Sometimes, when she rode the subway home alone and the train wasn't too crowded, she put on her headset and listened to one of her Sonny Rollins or Charlie Parker tapes. She loved jazz in any form and spent time in New York's jazz clubs whenever she could find someone in her family to take her.

She looked at her watch again. The train was almost at Seventy-second Street. She was going to make it, unless something dire happened.

She arrived at the appointed site in Central Park with plenty of time to spare. Of course, M'dear had arrived early. She and the other models were inside the trailer, and the girls were listening to her grandmother and laughing. M'dear was telling them about her recent trip to India and her ride on an elephant.

"Tell them about the baby elephant," Nichelle said, as she sat down beside her grandmother. "Tell them how he got so jealous of you. . . ."

The photographer's assistant opened the door and peeked inside. "Everybody's here, I see," she said. "Good. After you're all changed, I'll send in Brad to do your hair."

An assistant helped them into their pretty spring dresses. Nichelle loved hers, a red dress with little colored flowers, and wished she could keep it. Oh well, maybe when she was a big hotshot model.

Then Brad got started on their hair. When it was Nichelle's turn, he fluffed up her long curls and smiled.

"You have gorgeous hair, dear," he said. He took out a bottle of water and sprayed her whole head. Then he fluffed it with his fingers and let it dry naturally.

"Beautiful!" he said.

Nichelle glanced in the mirror and smiled. It was funny how a stylist could do the same thing she did every morning and yet her hair came out fantastic.

The makeup woman came in when he was finished and worked on their faces.

They emerged from the trailer to find a

makeshift platform covered with fake grass, several feet above the snow. There were even pretty white benches to sit on. The photographer's stylists had done an amazing job.

"Perfect!" the photographer called. "You're all beautiful! Take off your jackets. Sit down on the benches. Let's get started. Smile. Put the straw hat on. No, not like that. Tilt it a bit. Make it cocky. Yes, that's perfect. But you're smiling too much. Just a little smile, like you've got a wonderful secret that no one will ever know but you. Yes! That's it! Good! Great, in fact!"

Nichelle had no trouble thinking of a secret. She had lots of secret crushes on actors, singers, boys at school, all kinds of people. Today she allowed Michael Jordan to bring a secret smile to her lips.

Between shots, Nichelle and the other girls raced into the trailer until it was time to shoot again. There was lots of laughter, and Nichelle liked all the girls. Nobody seemed stuck-up or vain at all. Meeting new people was one of the best parts of modeling, and these girls were especially nice.

The photographer was ready again. Nichelle settled back onto her bench. Above her head, the bright sun shone down, providing warmth.

It was a good shoot, short, sweet, and very easy. When they were finished, they went back into the trailer to change into their regular clothes. M'dear told the story about the jealous baby elephant, and everybody laughed.

Chapter 4

I'll Bet a Purple Shoe and Raise You a Donut

"How was the photo shoot?" Barbie asked later that evening. They were seated in front of the computer in Nichelle's purple and white bedroom.

Nichelle's favorite color dominated the room. The covers on the twin beds were purple, and so were the curtains on the large bay window. The huge black-and-white African-inspired rug that covered most of the oak floor was a beautiful complement to the bedspreads. Nichelle had added oak frames on the walls that held photos of her friends and family. It was a perfect finishing touch.

Nichelle loved her room. Sometimes there was no place she'd rather be, like now, here with Barbie, doing this work, as the sounds of traffic and gentle laughter floated in from outside.

"The photo shoot was fun. I met some great people."

"I can't wait to see you in *Style*. That's amazing!"

"I know," Nichelle said. "I still can't believe it."

Nichelle leaned closer to the computer and typed in her password. Within seconds they were in cyberspace.

"We've got to be careful about this," she explained. "We can't even tell my mother that we're doing this project." Quickly, she explained to Barbie about the conversation she'd overheard outside her mother's office at City Hall. "And maybe," she added, "you shouldn't tell Shawn. He's definitely down as a big brother, but sometimes he blabs too much. Anyway," Nichelle continued, "this guy Curtis is a very important man. He's a developer and he's interested in building near the African Burial Ground. He might even be interested in building on top of the sacred ground — they really don't know where the boundaries are.

He contributed zillions to the mayor's campaign, and my mother's supposed to keep hands off on this project. She could lose her job."

"My lips are sealed," Barbie promised. "Where's your mom now?"

"She's at a meeting, and it should run late. My dad called and said he had to stay at the hospital until at least ten tonight. So we have plenty of time."

"And Shawn?" Barbie asked. "Where's he?"

"Basketball practice. Where else would he be when the Earth is covered with a blanket of snow? Inside, of course, preparing to lead the varsity basketball team to yet another winning season."

Nichelle clicked on the search button and typed in "New York City African Burial Ground." A list of twelve articles appeared. There were articles on the burial ground itself, the proposed memorial, artifacts, and a short history of slavery in the New York area.

"That's interesting," Nichelle said, pointing to an article entitled "Gravesite Objects." "I wonder what that is?" She clicked PRINT and waited as the pages slid from her printer.

"How about that one!" Barbie was pointing to an article called "Unearthing Our African Ancestry."

Nichelle printed out the article and several others, and gave half of them to Barbie.

"Our dear friend Mr. Curtis should take a look at this one!" said Barbie, reading a list of objects found in the burial ground. "Cups, vases, soap dishes, dolls' heads, false teeth. This place is a museum!

"It says here that the burial ground was unearthed in 1991, and that it extends about five or six acres. City Hall Park is right on top of it. And listen to this — when it was used in the 1700s, it wasn't even in the city limits of New York."

"Five or six acres," said Nichelle. "Wow. That's a big chunk of downtown. Almost anyplace you build down there might disturb the burial ground. I can see why people like Curtis don't want to deal with it."

"Look," Barbie said. "Here's a map. They were building a new federal building when they discovered it. By that time, it had been all covered over and built up for so long, nobody even knew it existed anymore."

Secrets of the Past

"All those people had been forgotten!" Nichelle sighed sadly. "The 1700s. That's 150 years before the Civil War. It says that one out of every five New Yorkers was a slave. Slave labor helped build this city. It also says they're discovering burial grounds in lots of other northern cities. And our not-so-up-to-date textbook doesn't even mention slavery in the North. That's incredible!"

"It is incredible," said Barbie. "So many people, and nobody even remembers them now."

"Hmmm?" Nichelle said without looking up. She was reading an article about a Native American burial site in New England. "Look at this," she said, engrossed. "They forced a delay on the building of a shopping mall. When some bones were found there, they got a court to say that the site had to be excavated before building could begin."

"It's really too bad we can't talk to your mother about the burial ground," said Barbie.

"It really is," said Nichelle. "But I'm starting to think that maybe we could do something to help her. Her hands are tied, but ours aren't."

"Maybe," said Barbie slowly, "this isn't just an extra-credit project for history."

Nichelle pretended not to hear Barbie. "Let's go

down there after school soon," Nichelle suggested. "We could do a little exploration and maybe even find out where Mr. Curtis is planning on putting up his building. If my mother's right, I'll bet it's too close for comfort!"

"Could Curtis be a problem?"

"He might be," Nichelle said gently, trying to sound reassuring. "He wants his building up fast, and he's a mover and a shaker. I've heard my mom talk about him before. He's given a lot of politicians a lot of money, and he expects something in return. And I'll bet my new blue overalls that this guy has no interest whatsoever in waiting until the borders of our African Burial Ground have been completely explored."

"I'll bet more than that!" Barbie laughed. "I'll bet my red and silver high heels that you're right."

"I'll bet my dog tags."

"And I'll raise you my palm tree charm!"

They were laughing hysterically now.

"Sunglasses!"

"History book!"

"Purple baseball cap!"

"Mr. Budge!"

"Glazed jelly donut with extra chocolate icing on top!"

They fell onto one of Nichelle's twin beds, laughing harder, until Nichelle shouted "Watch out Mr. Curtis! Nichelle and Barbie are on the case! And we won't sleep until those slaves can rest in peace!"

But they did sleep, of course, after Barbie had taken a yellow cab back to the Upper West Side and Nichelle had hidden all the research printouts under her sweaters in the bottom drawer of her dresser.

Chapter 5

Digging with Silver Teaspoons

The next afternoon, when sixth period was over, Nichelle went up to Room 712 and settled down to work on her math homework. Room 712 was everyone's favorite place. In this room the International High newspaper and website came to life. Ideas, some brilliant, some insane, were constantly being bounced around.

On this day, the small windowless room was a madhouse, as always. The floor was cluttered with bodies, chatting, studying, or merely sprawled out trying to catch a few ZZZZ's between classes. In one corner, a bunch of kids were scrunched over the computer, working on the newspaper's international website. In another, several students were huddled around a table, studying the proofs of the latest edition of the *I. H. Generation Beat.*

As always, Nichelle's math homework took her almost no time at all. When she finished, she opened her history book and attempted to read the assigned chapter. It was no use. She'd need a little peace and quiet if she was going to be able to understand it completely. She'd read it tonight in her room, where there was nothing to disturb her but the occasional sound of music drifting in from a neighbor's window.

There is a time and a place for everything, Nichelle thought. She loved this noisy loud newspaper room, but her room at home was very special. She had made it her own, and when she needed peace and quiet it was definitely the place to be.

She glanced at her watch. She had promised her friends that she would meet them across the street at Eatz when school was out. Eatz was the favorite place to eat for the kids who went to I. H. It was grubby and the food was a little strange, but it was definitely convenient.

Nichelle and her friends usually met there at

lunchtime, but today she had some last minute homework to do, so she had skipped lunch. Now she was starving.

She was walking out the door, when Mr. Toussaint stopped her.

"Hey, Nichelle!" he called from the other side of the madhouse.

Nichelle turned and made her way back through the stretched-out bodies.

"We're a little short on articles for the next issue," he said when she reached him. "Do you think you might be able to whip up about a thousand words about something interesting this week?" Nichelle was the fashion editor of the newspaper. It was her job to cover all the latest styles that appeared in the hallways of I.H. But now and then she'd write an article on whatever else interested her.

Whip up a thousand words. Sure, she hardly had anything to do.

Nichelle smiled wryly at him. "If I think of something I can do in about four seconds, I'll give it a try," she said.

"That's all I'm asking. Think about it, okay?" he said.

"I'm thinking, I'm thinking, I'm walking backwards," she said, backing out the door.

"Bye!" he said cheerfully.

When she walked into Eatz, Barbie, Chelsie, Ana, Lara, and Tori were crammed into their favorite orange vinyl booth in the far corner. They waved madly at her as she came through the door.

"Hey, Bill!" said Nichelle, waving as she went by the counter.

Bill, the cook, stuck his head through the small opening between the kitchen and the restaurant.

"Greetings, Nichelle!" he said with a friendly grin. "You fancy your usual?"

"Thanks, Bill," Nichelle told him. "But lots of cheese in my salad today, please. And mountains of olives, of course. I'm starving! Only olives will save my life!"

In a few minutes, Bill was standing beside her, holding a huge droopy-looking salad and a bottle of water.

"Sorry about the lettuce," he said. "It's a little dodgy today, but you'll survive."

"Why do I often feel like an outsider in my own country?" Nichelle laughed as she dug into her salad. "Dodgy? Here I am in Manhattan, being served by an Australian cook and sitting across from a Brit, a French-German-Italian, and another Australian. To say nothing of a Mexican-American and a girl from California, which might as well be another country."

"It's a nice country, though," said Barbie, taking no offense. Her friends knew that she often felt the same way about New York.

"Crikey," Chelsie said in her thickest British accent. "You wouldn't know what to do without us."

"Crikey, mate," Tori laughed, sounding like the Aussie she was. "If you hang around with us long enough, you won't be saying anything but 'crikey'!"

Nichelle unscrewed her bottle of water and took a long gulp. "This water's hot!" she called to Bill.

"I was afraid of that!" Bill called back. "It's been sittin' in the sun, workin' on a tan."

"It's freezing outside, mate!" Nichelle shouted, trying to mimic his Australian accent as she fingered the three small earrings in her left ear. "If it was outside it would have been frozen by now!"

"Who said anything about outside! I merely said it was sittin' in the sun on top of the oven. Come on, stop your moanin'. Hot water's good for you!"

"It is actually true," said Lara. "You know, they drink hot water in China all the time."

"How do you know stuff like that?" Ana asked her. It was true. Lara knew things about places all over the world. After all, she'd lived in half of them.

Nichelle groaned. "So guess what," she said, changing the subject with her friends. "Mr. Toussaint stopped me on the way out, and he asked me to write an extra article for the *Generation Beat*. Just a thousand words or so. Like I have time."

"Sure you do," grinned Ana. "Dinnertime. You don't have to eat, right?"

"Maybe," said Barbie, "you could do an article on . . . well, you know. The thing we're interested in." Nichelle knew that Barbie wouldn't let their secret slip, even to their best friends.

But of course, saying "well, you know" in front of their friends was like yelling "Fire!" in a crowded theater. Suddenly, four sets of eyes were totally riveted on Nichelle and Barbie.

"What?" said Ana. "What's 'well, you know'?"

"Come on," said Chelsie, "give."

Nichelle thought about it for a minute, and then she decided she could let their friends in on the secret. They knew when to keep their mouths shut.

"Okay," she said to them, "but you have to sit on this. No blabbing. It's important."

Nichelle began to explain. "Barbie and I are doing a project on slavery in the North, and we've been reading about the African Burial Ground near City Hall," she said.

"I didn't know there was a burial ground near City Hall," Chelsie said.

"Neither did I," Barbie told her.

"But what's the big secret?" Tori asked as she folded her arms on the table and leaned across toward Nichelle.

"It has to do with my mother's job," Nichelle explained. "I can't say any more than that, but my mother could lose her job if anyone finds out we're digging around down there."

Chelsie's back straightened as she stared at Nichelle. "What do you mean by 'digging around'?" she gasped. "You're not going down there in the middle of the night with shovels, are you?"

Barbie and Nichelle laughed out loud. "We're digging with teaspoons," Nichelle teased. "Tiny little silver ones. English silver. Only the best."

Chelsie stuck her tongue out at them and

grinned. "Okay," she said. "I shall not chat about this to anyone. In fact, the entire subject has, as of this moment, been erased from my mind."

"Thanks for understanding," said Nichelle.

"Understanding what?" asked Chelsie, deadpan. The others all shrugged, looking mystified.

Tori stood up and moved out of the booth. "Well," she said, "all I can say is, crikey! We'd better go, Chelsie, if you're coming with me. I have to get home."

After the others left, Barbie moved to the other side of the booth and faced Nichelle. "I have to go in a minute, too," she said. "Tons of homework. Some people aren't as lucky as you. Some people can't whip through their homework in seconds."

"Yeah, right," said Nichelle, laughing. But they both knew she was blessed with a fast mind and great focusing abilities.

Nichelle popped a Greek olive into her mouth, and offered Barbie one. "Hey," she said, "maybe it is a good idea to do a piece about the burial ground for Mr. Toussaint. We're both on the staff of the newspaper and website. You're the roving reporter, so we can rove. If we post it on the website, the whole world will be able to read about it. But we'll have to be careful what we say, to make sure my mom's job isn't in jeopardy."

They talked about it for a few minutes more and then got up, paid the bill, and left.

"I'll call you tonight!" Barbie shouted as she headed toward the West Side subway. "And say hello to Shawn. Tell him I'm in desperate need of his help in history."

"Will do!" Nichelle shouted. Then she waved, pulled up the collar on her coat, and turned the corner. Then she heard Barbie calling her one last time, and she screeched to a stop.

"Nichelle!" she was saying. "Do you want to go downtown and look around after school tomorrow?"

Nichelle poked her head around the corner. "Tomorrow's good, I think," she replied. "Call me tonight, okay?"

Chapter 6

Nichelle Spills the Beans

Shawn was sitting at the kitchen table when Nichelle got home. He was devouring a peanut butter sandwich and studying his chemistry book. He looked up as she went over to the refrigerator and poured herself a glass of juice.

"Pour me a glass, too," he said, grinning at her. "Please, little sister." He put up his hands to look like a begging puppy.

She poured another glass of juice and sat down across from him. He drank it in three gulps.

"By the way," Nichelle said, "Barbie needs tutoring. She told me to ask you when it would be convenient."

"This weekend, no problem," said Shawn, as he stood up and put his dish in the sink. "Tell her to call me."

Then he picked up the phone and carried it out of the room. "Shawn's appendage," they called the phone, because her brother was always using it. Every morning Nichelle's friends would say "I tried to call you last night, but I just got your voice mail." No matter what anyone did or said, Shawn usually spent hours on the phone.

"Can't we get call waiting?" Nichelle would ask her parents, but they always refused. Dr. Watson had his own phone and a beeper that was only available to his service or his patients, and the only other phone was "Shawn's appendage."

"My mother absolutely refuses to get call waiting!" Nichelle explained to her friends when they complained. "She hates it. My mom's attitude is we have voice mail. If the line is busy, the caller can leave a message and you can call back. No call waiting, no three-way-calling, and if she had her way we wouldn't have a phone at all. When she gets home from work at night, she wants things calm."

So, as usual, Shawn was on the phone all

evening. Nichelle knew that Barbie was probably trying to call her, and maybe her other friends were, too. But she had a lot of homework and several letters to write, so she didn't worry too much.

Just before she turned off her lamp, her mother stopped in to say goodnight. She sat on the bed beside Nichelle. "It's really sad that you're too big to read picture books to now," she said. "I miss it."

"You can still read to me," said Nichelle. "Good night brush and the bowl full of mush. . . ."

They both laughed. Nichelle climbed under the covers, and her mother kissed her on the forehead, just as she had when Nichelle was small.

"Mom," said Nichelle suddenly, "what would happen if I accidentally came upon some information about the African Burial Ground? Something that might stop . . . some person. Someone who might want to build there before it could be checked out?" The question had flown out of her mouth before she'd had time to stop it. Keeping things from her mom was just not in her nature.

Ms. Watson knitted her brows. "I thought I saw your shadow the other day," she said. "Did you hear that whole conversation?"

"Sort of," said Nichelle. "I sort of couldn't help it."

"Well, you should forget you heard it. This is not kid stuff."

Nichelle persisted. "But what if I accidentally found something that could help?"

Her mother turned out the lamp. "You have to do what your conscience dictates," she said just before she closed the door.

The next morning before her first class, Nichelle ran up to the fifth floor to see if there were any notes under the tile for her. She didn't know how she and her friends could survive if it weren't for the loose tile that they used as a place to leave secret messages for each other. Only the six of them knew it was there — it looked just like all the other tiles.

Carefully, Nichelle lifted the tile. Sure enough, there was a folded-up note in Barbie's pretty, round handwriting. "Nichelle," it said on the outside.

"I couldn't get through last night," it said, "but I wanted to tell you — I e-mailed my parents last night and told them that we had discovered an archaeological site. I asked them for some general advice about digging up artifacts, but I didn't give any details. Leave me a note!"

Of course, Barbie could have talked to Nichelle after Mr. Budge's class, but it was much more fun to leave notes in their secret hiding place.

Barbie must have gone off on some other errand, because when Nichelle got to Mr. Budge's class, Barbie wasn't there. Nichelle took her seat at the back of the room — only Patty Weir sat behind Nichelle. There was a whole three minutes before class started, and Nichelle decided to take full advantage of it. She put her headphones on and closed her eyes. For those few moments, she felt perfectly at peace with the world.

In a minute, Nichelle felt Barbie slide into the chair beside her. She opened one eye and grinned at her friend.

"I'm listening to Zoot," she said quietly. "And I'm happy."

Nichelle had introduced Barbie to Zoot Sims a few months earlier. He was a tenor sax player back in the 40s and 50s, and he was one of her favorites. Nichelle had even named a cat after him when she was a little girl.

"I got your note," Nichelle said, turning off the tape player and putting it away. She reached into her pack and pulled out Barbie's envelope. "Sorry you couldn't get through," she said. "Shawn was on the phone with his newest girlfriend."

"I sort of told my mother I knew about Mr. Curtis last night," said Nichelle.

There was a sharp intake of breath from Barbie. "What did she say?"

"She said that I should do whatever my conscience dictates."

"Which means?"

"Which means that she doesn't want to know about it, and that we should be careful."

Class was about to start. Mr. Budge was glaring at them. When they finally noticed, they smiled politely and stopped talking. After a moment, he turned his back and picked up the chalk that signaled yet another list. Nichelle scribbled a note to Barbie.

"I forgot to tell you," it said. "I was on the phone last night, too. Guess what! A woman from *Teen Style* Magazine called. She wants me on another shoot tomorrow afternoon, and you won't believe this: It's just me! They're doing an entire shoot around me! Can you believe it?"

Mr. Budge had some kind of sixth sense that told him when a note was being passed. He put down his chalk as precisely as a dentist puts down his favorite instrument. Then he raised the index finger of his right hand and shook it, very, very slowly, straight at Nichelle.

Chapter 7

The Man in Front of the Brownstone

When Nichelle and Barbie left the building that afternoon, the sun was shining brightly and the snow had melted. Nichelle pulled off her purple winter coat, tossed it over one shoulder, and belted out a song from *South Pacific,* changing the last word.

"I'm in love, I'm in love, I'm in love with a wonderful sky!" she sang.

"I love that show," Barbie said. "We put it on last year at Malibu High. I was one of the nurses."

Skipping along, enjoying the sun, they traded show tunes as they passed the World Trade Center, Trinity Church, City Hall, and headed down

Duane Street. They sang songs from *Sound of Music, South Pacific* and *Oklahoma*, from *Porgy and Bess, Rent,* and *Ragtime.*

Nichelle wondered what her life would be like without music. She loved all kinds of music very much — show tunes, rap, jazz, rhythm & blues, classical, and rock 'n' roll. She just couldn't begin to imagine life without music.

They were in the middle of a song from *Grease,* when they turned a corner, and found themselves facing the large Federal Office Building at 290 Broadway.

"Part of the burial ground is right under that huge building!" Nichelle said. "Isn't that incredible? All that history right under our feet!"

Nichelle and Barbie walked into the Federal Office Building and looked around. There was a large unfinished space on the ground floor. "I think the plans call for this area to be the interpretive center," Nichelle whispered, glancing at the printout she'd brought along. "It'll be kind of like a museum. Oh, and look over there. If you look out the window, you can see where the memorial's going to be."

"And what will that be like?" asked Barbie, looking out at the large fenced-off area.

"Well," Nichelle whispered, reading the information from the website, "right now, the remains of about four hundred people are in Washington, D.C., at Howard University. They're doing research on them. It says that when the research is done, the remains will be reburied out here, in the memorial. There's going to be a beautiful park."

Nichelle took out her camera and snapped several pictures.

"Did you bring your video camera?" she whispered when she was finished.

Barbie nodded. "Do you think I should use it in here?" she asked.

"Maybe we shouldn't be taking pictures in here," Nichelle said, putting her camera away. "Let's go outside."

Barbie followed Nichelle out the front door and over to the proposed memorial site.

"I think you can film here," Nichelle said, but she wasn't completely sure. She wanted to document this historic site for their project, but she also wanted to be respectful. She was thinking about the people who might still be buried there. "I guess it's all right," she said after a moment.

Barbie took out her video camera and turned it

on. She filmed for about three minutes without saying a word, then put it away.

"Let's see if we can find Curtis's fiasco," Nichelle suggested when Barbie was finished. She had seen a map on her mother's desk at home, so she knew exactly where it was. They hurried down Elk Street and turned a corner. After walking a little farther, they stopped in front of a construction site. The sun was beginning to set now, and the air was cooler. Nichelle slid into her coat and buttoned it.

"This must be it," she told Barbie as they moved toward the chain-link fence that protected the site from potential intruders.

"It's so . . ." Barbie hesitated, searching for the right word. "I don't know . . . incomplete, I guess."

"I'd call it 'not even started,'" Nichelle added as she pulled out her camera and snapped a picture.

There was nothing on the lot beyond the chain-link fence — nothing but a gaping expanse of damp dirt and rocks, a few mounds of melting snow, and a sign that said "Curtis Development Co. Site of the CURTIS COMPOUND, Lower Manhattan's Newest Office and Residential Tower."

Barbie turned on her camera and began to shoot. "Do you know what was here before?"

Barbie asked as she turned slowly, taking in the entire site.

She stopped suddenly, and kept her camera pointed in one direction, and when she failed to move, Nichelle walked closer and tried to focus on what Barbie was seeing.

"What is it?" Nichelle asked.

Barbie pushed the 'zoom' button, without moving, barely breathing.

"What!" Nichelle cried.

"There's a man over there in front of that old brownstone. He's watching us."

"What does he look like?"

Barbie zoomed in even closer. "He's huge! He's wearing a suit and tie, and he's carrying a clipboard. He's got a pencil behind his ear, and Nichelle —"

"Oh, boy!" Nichelle gasped. "Let me guess! He's coming this way, right?"

"Right!" Barbie lowered the video camera and stared nervously at her friend. In a few seconds the man was beside them.

"Why are you here?" he demanded. "What are you videotaping?" He was standing quite close to them, and he towered over them both.

Secrets of the Past

In front of the brownstone, the girls noticed a long black limousine pulling up to the curb. The driver climbed out. "Ready when you are, Mr. Curtis!" he called.

"Are you *the* Mr. Curtis," Barbie asked nervously. "The man with the sign?"

"That's right. And you didn't answer my question."

"Tourists," Nichelle said quickly, trying to sound nonchalant. "We're tourists. Just taking a few pictures of our trip to New York. We're from California. Nice place, California. Sunny most of the year, but sometimes in the winter it gets quite cold. Fine state, California. Lots of oranges."

Curtis just stared at them. Then he cleared his throat, sighed an annoyed sigh, and stomped back toward the brownstone.

"Whew!" said both girls together when he was out of earshot.

"Just remember," said Nichelle softly, "we haven't done anything illegal. Don't let him scare you. I wonder what he's doing at that brownstone?"

As Barbie and Nichelle watched, he knocked on the door of the brownstone, and when it opened he started to shout. The man in the doorway listened for a minute, then slammed the door in Curtis's face.

"I wonder what that was about," Barbie said, shading her eyes from the sun's glare.

"Maybe we should pay a visit to whoever lives there," Nichelle suggested.

"Maybe we should," Barbie agreed, lowering her hand and turning toward her friend. "Maybe we should."

Chapter 8

A Grave Undertaking

After the door slammed, Mr. Curtis stomped to the limousine at the curb, then hesitated and glanced over at them. The sun was starting to set behind him, making it difficult to read the expression on his face, but Nichelle and Barbie could guess.

Mr. Curtis was not happy. He waited as the driver opened the door for him. Then, as he leaned down and climbed inside, he took one last backward glance at them and shook his huge, balding head.

"Well," Nichelle said as the limo pulled away. "Man, that was scary. I wonder what he's going to do."

"My guess is that he's only interested in getting that building finished. He won't be thrilled with anything that gets in his way."

"Like us," Nichelle interrupted.

"Like us," Barbie agreed.

They both gulped.

Barbie and Nichelle walked over to the brownstone and knocked. An elderly African-American man yanked the door open angrily.

"I thought I told you —" he shouted.

When he realized that two girls were standing before him, he hesitated and smiled a welcoming smile.

"Sorry," he said politely. "I thought you were someone else."

"Like Mr. Curtis?" Nichelle laughed.

"You saw him?"

"That's right."

The old man sighed and extended his hand. "Hi, my name is Ed Brook. That monster wants me to sell him my house!" he explained. "My house! I've lived in this house all my life. It's my home. My parents lived here before me. My grandparents lived here. I wouldn't be surprised if some of my ancestors are buried right under our feet. And now

Secrets of the Past

Curtis wants me to give it up so that he can build another obscene high-rise. Well, I refuse! He's never going to get my house. He can come here in person all he wants. His lawyers can write me letters. He can try all the dirty, underhanded tricks he wants. I'll tell you, I wish there was some way I could fix his wagon!"

"Maybe there is," Nichelle told him. "And I think the burial ground is our key. I'll bet if we can find one small artifact on his property, or at least on your property right near his, then he'll have to wait until the archaeologists get done excavating it."

"And delay costs money," the elderly man agreed.

"I don't even feel bad for him," said Nichelle as Barbie nodded in agreement. "He's a bully, and he pushes people around."

The old man grinned.

"I guess we'd have to dig," Nichelle explained. "We'd have to dig until we find an artifact that will prove the burial ground extends into Curtis's site. Then we'd have to submit it to the city."

"I'm a little old for digging." Mr. Brook laughed. "But you girls can dig on my land all you want. There are even some places where the fence is kind of broken, if you catch my meaning. So it might be a little hard to know exactly whose land you're digging up. Could be mine, could be his."

The old man smiled at Nichelle. "There are lots of interesting things down there," he continued. "Buttons, rings, coins, beads. Where there are graves there are artifacts. Good luck to you. But you'd better dig only in the mornings. Curtis comes around afternoons to gaze lovingly at his land and yell at me. But he's a late sleeper and he's never here before noon."

Barbie and Nichelle thanked Ed Brook and promised to return early the next morning. Then they walked over to City Hall and took the subway home with Nichelle's mother. They talked about school, and the newspaper, and Nichelle's modeling job, but no one mentioned Mr. Curtis or the burial ground. Nichelle thought it was kind of odd since that was the main thing on everyone's mind.

"Will you stay for dinner?" Ms. Watson asked Barbie as the train pulled into the station. "We'll stop at a few stores and you can help me pick out something delicious to cook."

"I'll have to call Sam and Terri first, but I'd love to," Barbie said. "The best things about New York are all the little food stores. In California, we usually go to the supermarket. This is more fun."

After Barbie called, they stopped at the bakery, where they bought some olive bread and a loaf of fresh rye. Then they stopped at a deli for three kinds of olives to make Nichelle happy, and two kinds of large dill pickles, and four kinds of cheese; "the smellier the better," Nichelle said.

They bought fruits and vegetables at a different shop, and when they were laden down with packages and almost home, Mrs. Watson turned to Barbie and said, "So, what is your pleasure, meat or fish? Or are you a vegetarian? I can't remember."

"My mother calls me her anything-goes food fanatic," Barbie laughed. "That's because I'll eat anything — vegetables, meat, fish — everything except beets and anchovies. I have a hard time with anchovies."

They stopped at the fish store and bought some sole, and then they went home and cooked up a feast. It was just the three of them, because Dr. Watson was still at the hospital and Shawn was at basketball practice.

The meal was delicious.

When they were finished, Nichelle and Barbie

did the dishes and then went up to Nichelle's room to use the computer. Barbie signed on as a guest and checked her mail. There was a letter from her parents.

"Listen to this," Barbie said, as she read the e-mail.

As for your questions about determining the dates of artifacts, let's start with human remains — skulls for instance.

"Skulls?" Nichelle said. It hadn't occurred to her that they might dig up something so real!

Barbie continued reading.

We can tell how old a skull is through radiocarbon dating. All living things contain carbon. The carbon in a dead body disintegrates slowly, so we can tell how long it has been dead by measuring it. When we're digging in what we think is a graveyard and we find a cup or a doll, we assume there may be a body nearby. So we dig some more. If there is no body or skull anywhere in the vicinity, then all we probably have is a cup or a doll that was recently thrown there. Hope this has been helpful for your report or whatever you need it for. Good luck!

"Carbon!" Nichelle said. "That's fascinating! I wonder what we'll find there. Dolls and cups? That is so incredible!" She was imagining the families that might have used those buried objects.

Barbie grinned happily and sat back in her chair. "I can't wait!" she said. "What if we're digging away and we find a bone and it's radiocarbon dated back to the 1700s? That would be amazing!"

"I'll settle for a button," Nichelle said. "That's all we need to show that Curtis is trying to build on the burial ground."

Barbie stood up and stretched her arms above her head. Then she touched her toes three times. "I can't wait!" she said again. "Shall we meet at the Curtis Compound at, say, nine tomorrow morning? We don't have school tomorrow, remember? It's teachers' conference day. For once we get off, and the rest of the city works!"

"We should make it earlier," Nichelle said. "To have enough time in case Curtis comes again. How about six-thirty? That should give us plenty of time to dig. I still have the shovels we used for the neighborhood garden, so I'll bring them. I guess we'd better get to bed. I have that photo shoot tomorrow afternoon, so I need my beauty sleep."

They walked outside together. The night was

chilly but the sky was an inverted bowl of brightly lit stars. It wasn't often that you saw stars like that above Manhattan. The girls studied them with awe.

"Just think of it, Barbie," Nichelle said softly. "About 250 years ago our ancestors were staring up at these very same stars. Isn't that incredible?"

Barbie didn't answer. She was too busy admiring the constellations, just as their grandmothers and grandmother's grandmothers had probably done a long, long time before.

Chapter 9

A Treasure from the Past

Nichelle was so excited about the dig that she arrived fifteen minutes early. She saw Barbie approaching, way down the block, and waited for her.

When she reached Nichelle's side, Mr. Brook had already opened his front door.

"Hello, Mr. Brook! Hello, Barbie!" Nichelle said. "You would not believe the looks I got from the people on the subway because I was carrying these shovels!" she giggled. "This is Manhattan, after all, and there aren't many reasons for carrying two long garden tools around at dawn in November."

A Sonny Rollins solo was drifting out through the front door.

"I love him!" Nichelle said. "Do you like jazz?"

"Come inside and see for yourself," he said, grinning. "I'll put the kettle on."

Nichelle and Barbie followed the old man into the brownstone. When Mr. Brook went into the kitchen, Nichelle wandered over to the shelf that held Mr. Brook's record collection. There were stacks and stacks of jazz LPs, and many of the record sleeves and album jackets seemed to be in mint condition.

"This is amazing!" she called.

"What's that?" Mr. Brook called back.

"Your records! Do you mind if I look through them?"

"Sure. Go right ahead. Some of them go back to when I was a boy."

Nichelle couldn't believe what this man had in his collection. There were early Miles Davis records, and she couldn't believe it when she saw he had an early Zoot LP!

"Sit down, sit down," Mr. Brook said as he came back into the small living room. He was carrying a tray on which were cups of steaming tea and a heaping plate of muffins and butter and jam.

"So you like my music?" Ed Brook said as he handed Nichelle a cup of tea.

"I love your music!" she said as she sat down and sipped the tea.

"What would you like to hear?"

"Zoot's my favorite," Nichelle told him.

"Mine, too!" Mr. Brook said as he stood and walked to the record shelf. He placed the LP gently on the turntable and sat back down.

As Zoot's powerful music filled the room, Nichelle looked around her. She had been so busy searching through the records that she hadn't noticed the wonderful treasures in Mr. Brook's small neat room. The walls were covered with black and white photographs and wonderful drawings of landscapes and faces and buildings. Nichelle put down her cup and went across the room to study one of the photos. It was a photo of a very old man.

"That's my grandfather," Mr. Brook said. "All of the photos are of my relatives. Most of them are dead now, but it's so good to have them there on my walls all day long. They're my family, you know, no matter where they are.

"Can you tell me about these?" Nichelle asked as she moved on to the drawings.

Mr. Brook laughed. "Since they came from my hand, I certainly can. I do a little drawing. I'm not very good, but I like to draw things that are important to me. That building, for example, is where I grew up, and that field is what I remember from visiting my grandfather. But the faces, well, as I said, the faces of my loved ones are what I carry around in my soul, and sometimes I just have to let them out and put them down on paper."

Nichelle hesitated in front of a drawing of a little girl.

"That's my oldest daughter," Ed Brook said. "She's a lot bigger than that now. She's got a couple of kids of her own, but she moved out to California."

"That's where I'm from," Barbie said.

They chatted some more, and then the subject turned to the morning's business. "I sure hope you'll find something down there," said Mr. Brook.

Nichelle sat down and buttered a muffin. "I keep thinking about the people who are buried in that graveyard," she said. "I keep picturing what their lives must have been like. What songs they sang, what stories they told."

"I know," Mr. Brook agreed. "It's one of the reasons that I love living right here. I think about those people all the time."

They ate their muffins without speaking, listening to Zoot, and when they were finished, Barbie and Nichelle stood and thanked Mr. Brook for the snack. Then they went outside and walked over to the chain-link fence.

It was a special time of day in Manhattan for Nichelle. She loved the early mornings. It was too early for the streets to be filled with commuters, and the traffic was light. This particular morning was quiet and soft and gentle as she plunged in her shovel and dug into the ground. They worked very close to Mr. Brook's side of the fence. On Curtis's land, they could see the rubble that remained of the old garage that had occupied the lot.

They dug in the hard soil as the sun rose in the sky and the winter morning air warmed. They were about to give up when Nichelle felt something hard. She dropped her shovel and fell to her knees, scraping the dirt with her fingernails.

"What is it?" Barbie shouted. "Did you find something?" She ran over to Nichelle.

Nichelle pointed to a strange-looking gray object.

"What is that?" asked Barbie.

"I'd guess it's the bone of an animal," Nichelle said. "Maybe it's a cat's bone or maybe a dog's."

She remembered reading that people used to bury pets and people in the same graveyard. If this was a bone from the 1700s, maybe they had found a way to stop Curtis.

"Make sure you videotape this," said Nichelle. "Tape it while it's still in the ground, and then as I take it out, okay? And I'll take still photos."

"You got it," said Barbie as Nichelle began to carefully clean the dirt from around the bone. Then she put the bone gently aside.

With a renewed sense of purpose, she dug in again. And after an hour, she found something else hidden in the dirt.

"Barbie! Come look!" she yelled.

"It looks like a vase of some kind," Barbie said, joining her friend. She leaned down and taped Nichelle pulling it out of the ground. "It's so old!

Careful, it's practically falling apart! Wow, it's really long."

"That's just what I was noticing," said Nichelle thoughtfully. "And look where I found it. Half of it is on Mr. Brook's land. . . ."

"And half is on Curtis's!" screamed Barbie, immediately clapping her hand over her mouth.

"We should get it to somebody official immediately!" Nichelle said excitedly. "Together with the bone, this could be definite proof!"

"Who?" Barbie asked.

Nichelle glanced at her watch. "I guess it's time to talk to my mom. When you finish taping everything, let's go over there."

When Barbie was finished documenting their findings, they left their shovels with Mr. Brook and wrapped their treasures in the clean clothes they had brought to change into. When the vase and the bone were safely packed in Nichelle's backpack, they raced up to City Hall.

"Are you scared?" Barbie asked as they walked.

"Umm . . . yes," said Nichelle. "Maybe I should practice what I'm going to say to her."

So she practiced sounding very reasonable as

Barbie pretended to be Mrs. Watson. But as soon as they got there, excitement overtook Nichelle, and the reasonable speech went out the window.

"You won't believe!" Nichelle cried breathlessly, as she burst through the doorway of her mother's office.

Mrs. Watson glanced up and frowned. Nichelle and Barbie skidded to a stop and looked around them. Five men were watching them with eyes filled with curious bemusement.

"Welcome," one of them said. Nichelle recognized him as Mr. Evans, the man who had threatened her mother in the hallway.

"Mom!" Nichelle pleaded, ignoring him. "Could we talk to you for a moment, please. It's really important!"

Ms. Watson pushed back her chair, excused herself, and followed Nichelle and Barbie out into the hall.

"This had better be important!" she whispered, when they were at the other end of the hallway. "That was a crucial meeting about landmarking a neighborhood in Brooklyn."

Nichelle gently pulled the vase and the bone out of her pack and handed them to her mother.

"We dug these up next to the Curtis compound," she whispered. "The vase was partly under the compound. We think they might be from the African Burial Ground, which would mean he couldn't put up that building, right?"

"You did what?" Mrs. Watson cried. She sounded excited, concerned, and more than a little annoyed.

"We dug them up," Nichelle said. "I mean, we're not great archaeologists or anything, but the bulldozers were going to get it all anyway! Radio-carbon testing should show how old that bone is, right?"

Mrs. Watson's face softened. "This is incredible!" she agreed. "Where exactly did you find them?" Clearly, the idea that they might have the proof they needed to stop Curtis had swept away her annoyance.

Nichelle smiled a relieved smile. She had been afraid that her mother would be furious. "There's a nice little brownstone next to Curtis's site. A man called Ed Brook lives there."

"Sure. I know Ed. We've had many conversations. What about him?"

"He'll show you exactly where we found it," Nichelle told her.

Mrs. Watson put one arm around her daughter, the other around Barbie, and gave them a big hug.

"I'll have these tested today. There's no time to go through the normal channels. We should know pretty soon. I'll tell you the results the minute I hear anything."

Grinning proudly, the girls started skipping down the long, wide corridor. They were halfway to the stairs when Mrs. Watson called to them.

"Oh, and by the way, you might want to stop in that women's room at the end of the hall and wash up. You're looking a little grubby."

Nichelle and Barbie smiled and waved and raced into the women's room. When Nichelle looked in the mirror she could hardly believe her eyes. Grubby was an extreme understatement.

"Yuck!" Nichelle groaned. "And we've used our change of clothes to wrap up the artifact!"

Chapter 10

A Perfect Day

Nichelle and Barbie discussed shower possibilities and settled on Lara's, because it was the closest to City Hall.

Nichelle washed her hands in the City Hall sink, peered into the mirror, and laughed. "We're so dirty they'll throw us off the train!"

Lower Manhattan was coming alive as they hurried to the subway station. No one tossed them off the train because they were dirty, but they did get a few odd looks from some of the well-dressed stock brokers on their way to work. At first Nichelle felt embarrassed, but then she remembered why she was dirty, and she decided to concentrate on that.

"Think about it, Barbie," she said. "If that bone is as old as we hope it is, well, it will be absolutely amazing."

A well-dressed man across the aisle was frowning at them. Nichelle was tempted to tell him about the shovels and the vase and the bone that they hoped was from the 1700s, but she decided not to. It was still a secret, after all.

At nine o'clock they were banging on Lara's door.

Lara pulled the door open sleepily and gasped when she saw them.

"What happened to you two!" she cried. "You look like you've been playing in the dirt!"

Nichelle smiled. "Something like that," she said. "But I'm not sure I'd call it playing. Can we come in?"

"Sure," Lara said. "Chelsie's here. She slept over last night. Isn't it great to have a day off from school?"

Lara led Nichelle and Barbie into her bedroom and plopped down on the extra bed beside Chelsie. Chesie groaned and turned over. She opened her eyes slowly, noticed the grimy girls who were standing above her, and sat up straight.

"What in the world happened to you two!" she asked, rubbing her eyes.

"We had a little dirty business to take care of," Nichelle said, laughing. She turned to Lara. "Mind if we use your shower?"

"Please do," Lara laughed.

"But when you're done," added Chelsie, "you'd better tell us what's going on here. Or does it have something to do with the big secret? I know, you've been digging in the African Burial Ground with tiny little silver teaspoons, right?"

Nichelle laughed and headed for the shower. "We'll tell you all about it," she called as she turned on the water. "The whole thing is too cool for words!"

Nichelle told Chelsie and Lara about the vase while Barbie was in the shower. Then she swore them to secrecy.

"I could eat a mountain!" said Lara. "How about some breakfast? My mother left early this morning, so we have the kitchen to ourselves."

Lara whipped up a batch of blueberry pancakes, and the girls gathered around Lara's big wooden kitchen table and devoured them. The pancakes were wonderful.

"You're amazing, Lara!" Barbie said between bites. "You can do anything."

"Barbie's right," Nichelle agreed. "These pancakes are delicious. I didn't know you were an artist in the kitchen, too."

"Brilliance, how you say, oozes from my fingertips," Lara said jokingly. "Everyting I touch turns into a work of art."

"Oh, please!" Nichelle groaned. "You may be artistic, but let's not get carried away here!"

"I'll do the washing up," Chelsie said when they were finished, but Lara insisted on helping, and so did Barbie and Nichelle. As they worked, Nichelle shifted her mind to her upcoming photo shoot.

"I'd better get some rest before this afternoon," she said as she hung up the dish towel. "Believe it or not, I forgot all about the shoot for a little while because of the bone."

"The bone?" Chelsie cried. "What bone!"

Nichelle laughed and slipped on her jacket. "I guess I forgot to mention the bone. But don't worry," she told her friend. "We'll tell you every single detail sooner or later."

Nichelle said good-bye and closed the door softly behind her.

Maybe she'd walk for awhile. She had plenty of time. It was nice to have time to herself, for a change.

She walked for about a half hour before she took the subway up to Harlem. It was turning into a beautiful crisp day and she wanted to enjoy it. For some reason she didn't really feel tired, which was strange since she had been up since five. Maybe it was Lara's pancakes or the excitement of finding the vase and the bone.

She just kept on smiling. She smiled all the way uptown and couldn't help noticing that people on the subway smiled back at her. It was nice.

When she got home she went up to her room and lay down on her bed. She was still smiling as she fell asleep, and when she woke up a few hours later she still felt happy.

Her grandmother rang the doorbell an hour and a half before it was time for the photo shoot to begin. Nichelle was dressed and ready.

"It's a beautiful day," M'dear said happily. "I walked all the way up here."

Nichelle's grandmother usually liked to take the bus. "I prefer the great outdoors," M'dear would say when Nichelle suggested they take the subway. "I like to watch the people and feel the sun."

Nichelle was ready. They rode the bus downtown together, and when they arrived at the park, the sun was shining brightly and everyone seemed glad to see them.

The photographer's assistant greeted them and led them into the trailer. When M'dear was settled, the hair stylist came in and helped Nichelle with her hair, and then the makeup artist worked on her face.

"We've got some beautiful spring clothes for you to model today," the assistant told her, "shorts and T-shirts and a sweet pink dress."

Nichelle shivered. It was a lovely sunny day, but it was still winter, after all.

The assistant seemed to understand. "Don't worry," she laughed. "You won't be standing around in the cold. We'll set everything up before you come out of this nice warm trailer. You'll only be outside for a few minutes."

The shoot was as perfect as the rest of the day had been. Everyone was nice to her, and when it was over they complimented her on her attitude.

"You're a joy," the assistant said. "We'll call you again very soon."

"She's right, you know," M'dear told her as they were walking out of the park. "You are a joy. You'll be getting many more calls, if you want them."

"I do want them, M'dear," Nichelle said. "I love modeling."

M'dear took Nichelle's hand and squeezed it. "I can tell," she said. "And the camera loves you. I can't wait to see the pictures."

"Are you still coming on Sunday?" Nichelle asked. "Everyone's going to be there. Shawn has promised not to even touch a basketball, and Dad says he's made arrangements for someone to cover his emergencies."

M'dear laughed. "I wouldn't miss this for anything in the world," she said. "This is quite the occasion."

And what an occasion it was! Everyone kept their promise. Dr. Watson's beeper did not go off once, and Nichelle's mother unplugged the phone so that Shawn and Nichelle could devote all of their attention to the family.

It was a perfect day. Nichelle built a fire in the

living room fireplace, while her parents made a complete southern meal from scratch. They had potato salad, cornbread, greens, and roast beef. And after dinner they played all kinds of board games and Nichelle beat her father and brother half the time.

Chapter 11

On Your Feet, Barbie and Nichelle!

"How's the article on the African Burial Ground coming along?" Mr. Toussaint asked a few days later. Nichelle and Barbie were sprawled out on the floor of Room 712 finishing up their biology homework.

Nichelle and Barbie had told him as much of the story as they could after their big discovery at the Curtis Compound, and he'd been very excited about it. They had decided to write the piece together. But they still weren't able to tell him everything.

"It's on hold," Nichelle told him. "We're still waiting for test results."

"Tests?"

Nichelle nodded but didn't say any more. She knew she appeared secretive, but she couldn't explain about the radiocarbon test that should have been completed on that bone. Not yet anyway. Not while Mr. Curtis didn't know what they'd found.

It had been more than a week since they had discovered the bone and the vase. For the first few days, Nichelle had pleaded with her mother to call, write, beg, borrow, and steal in order to get the results of the test faster, but Mrs. Watson had just laughed.

"Obviously you don't understand the workings of the New York City lab," she had said. "You can scream and holler all you want, but it won't do any good. They'll finish when they finish, Nichelle, so have patience."

Nichelle had agreed to try, and as the days passed, she began to forget about the radiocarbon test. Except that Mr. Toussaint kept asking her about it.

"We should be able to finish it soon," was all she

could say. And Mr. Toussaint seemed to accept that, but Nichelle was beginning to worry how long that reason would hold.

Nichelle finished her homework and walked over to City Hall to meet her mother. The door to Mrs. Watson's office was closed when she arrived, so she tossed her backpack onto the floor of the hallway and sat down beside it.

I hope this isn't going to be a long meeting, Nichelle thought. She was exhausted. There was too much going on lately, too much homework and too many shoots. She needed a good night's sleep.

The soft sound of footsteps moving back and forth through the long hallways of City Hall had a hypnotizing effect, and before long Nichelle was sound asleep with her head on her pack and her body curled up in the fetal position. Had she been awake, she could have watched the sun disappear behind the windows and the hallway become bathed in soft, mysterious shadows.

Nichelle was drifting into a strange dream filled with all kinds of mixed-up images: Ed Brook was there, and someone was playing the sax, and Mr. Curtis was holding a pen and an easel, and when

Nichelle looked she saw that he was drawing a picture of huge gray cat with sleepy red eyes, and as Curtis sketched away the cat opened his mouth and said something that sounded like "no" or maybe it was "more."

Nichelle sat up with a start. As she looked around, trying to understand where she was, the door to her mother's office burst open and Mr. Evans rushed out angrily. He was so anxious to get away that he didn't notice Nichelle stretched out on the floor below him.

He tripped over Nichelle's backpack, and caught himself just before he tripped over Nichelle. Startled, she slid backward into the wall.

"Oh, great!" Mr. Evans snapped gruffly as he straightened up. "Just what I need! An adolescent camping in the halls of City Hall! Don't you have anywhere else to sleep, young lady?"

Nichelle apologized and jumped to her feet, but Mr. Evans wasn't interested. He dismissed her with an annoyed wave of his hand and stomped away.

A few seconds later, Mrs. Watson came out, followed by the mayor of New York. At first he didn't see Nichelle either. He was too busy smiling and shaking her mother's hand.

"I think you know my daughter," Mrs. Watson said.

The mayor turned and greeted Nichelle warmly. "You should be proud of your mother," he said. "She seems to have saved one of New York's most important historical sites."

"The bone? Was it the bone?" Nichelle screeched. "The bone proved it?"

"That's right," Ms. Watson laughed. "The radio-carbon tests proved that it was the bone of a dog that had been there since the 1700s. I'm sure they'll find lots of other bones buried there, too."

"Yahoo!" Nichelle shouted as she jumped up and down.

The mayor seemed puzzled, as if this young woman had gone a little crazy right there in the middle of City Hall.

Mrs. Watson laughed louder. "You see, Mayor," she explained. "Nichelle and her friend were the ones who discovered that bone. They are the heroes, or culprits — depending on how you look at it — who saved the burial ground. They dug up that bone and brought it here and waited patiently for the results. They're the ones to thank."

"I thank you," the mayor said. "City Hall thanks

you. The people of New York thank you. I just wish this had been brought to my attention sooner."

"What about Mr. Curtis?" Nichelle asked, a bit sarcastically. "I bet he won't thank me."

The mayor smiled. "No, I doubt if he'll thank you, but that's all right. He'll have a choice: wait until the site is excavated, or build elsewhere. If I know my friend Curtis, by next week he'll be applying for a permit to build another building somewhere else. He's, shall we say, resourceful. And as for Mr. Evans, well, we'll be having a little talk about his extremely unprofessional behavior."

The mayor thanked Nichelle again and started to walk back toward his office.

"We're going to be giving a presentation about all this to our class," Nichelle called. "And we were wondering if, well, maybe, you'd like to come. It should be pretty interesting."

"When is it?" the mayor asked.

"Friday! Friday at eight-thirty in the morning. Mr. Budge's history room at International High."

"I'll be there," the mayor promised. "But where I go, so goes the press. You'd better move it to the auditorium."

Secrets of the Past

When Nichelle got home, she went straight to the phone, called Barbie, and told her the news. "Eight-thirty Friday morning," she said.

"Are you crazy? Friday? That's only three days away. We have so much homework, and now we have to put a whole multimedia presentation together in three days!"

"We can do it!" Nichelle laughed. "We are woman! Hear us roar! Can you come over and get started now? My neighbor has some kind of editing thing that we can borrow. It attaches to the computer, and then we just hook up your camera and run your videotape —"

"I'm on my way!" Barbie interrupted. "Pour me a soft drink, and I'll be there before the ice cubes melt."

Barbie and Nichelle worked at the computer until eleven o'clock that night. By the time they were finished, they had the first draft of a script for their "multimedia extravaganza" that would include, if and when they ever finished, slides, film clips, and lots and lots of brilliant, hysterical dialogue presented by both of them in turn.

Nichelle had her film developed the next day,

and that night, Wednesday, they stayed up until midnight, splicing it all together.

Thursday night, the last night before their presentation, they took turns standing in a corner of Nichelle's bedroom, practicing.

"We have to keep the tension up," Nichelle suggested after she had practiced explaining the history of the African Burial Ground. "Let's make it a mystery — you know will they or won't they save the day. That kind of thing."

"Okay, try it again."

Nichelle spoke about their trip downtown, and the moment when they noticed the brownstone. She hesitated.

"Do I sound mysterious?"

"I'm on the edge of my seat," Barbie laughed.

"Now you have to run the bone film," Nichelle said. "And I'll make everyone wonder what kind of bone it is. Is it a pig? Could it be a giraffe?"

They took a break and Nichelle called Chelsie. "Hey," she said when her friend answered. "I'm just calling to see how you're feeling."

"I'm feeling just fine," Chelsie said. "Why?"

"I just want to make sure you aren't sick or anything."

"I'm fine, Nichelle. Why?"

"I guess I'm calling to make sure you'll all be there in the morning. Barbie and I need you. Do you know where you'll be sitting?"

Chelsie laughed. "I'm beginning to understand," she said. "We'll try and get there early so we can sit up front, okay? Are you feeling a little shaky?"

"I guess so," Nichelle admitted. "Scared is more like it. Well, good night. Don't oversleep or anything."

By midnight Nichelle and Barbie were so tired that they could hardly keep their eyes open. Barbie spent the night at Nichelle's house, and the next morning they left for school by seven. They had a lot of work to do before the mayor and the press arrived in the school auditorium.

Chapter 12

You're on a Roll, Nichelle Watson!

Nichelle glanced down at the crowd gathered in the auditorium and shivered. Her heart was pounding in her ears like some huge bass drum: *boom, boom, boom.* For some reason she was terrified. She had given speeches before, and she had performed in plays, but this was different. This was the big time.

The room was overflowing with people. As soon as word had gotten out that the mayor would be attending a talk about the "most recent findings regarding the African Burial Ground," the thing had turned into a circus.

Nichelle couldn't understand why she was so

nervous. She had no trouble in front of a camera. Maybe it was because she had to make a speech in front of the mayor of New York and a crowd of newspaper reporters.

The plan was for Nichelle to introduce the program, and then Barbie would show her film. Nichelle would finish up when everyone was wondering how the "mystery" would end.

Nichelle smiled down at her mother, who was seated in the front row with M'dear, Shawn, the mayor, and several men in suits and ties. It was just too bad that her dad had to be on call that morning.

The press was gathered in small clusters on the other side of the auditorium. Some were carrying cameras, some had small tape recorders, and a few had pencils and notebooks. Nichelle guessed that each cluster represented a different newspaper or magazine, and that thought made her even more nervous.

What was she doing here?

Why in the world had she ever started this?

Where were her friends? Her support system?

She studied the room, searching for Lara and Chelsie and Ana and Tori, but she couldn't see them anywhere.

Where were they?

And then she heard them shouting her name from somewhere in the back of the auditorium. They must have arrived too late to get seats down front.

"Nichelle! Nichelle!" Ana hollered. "Back here!"

Nichelle noticed them then, jumping up and down in the back row, waving their arms at her.

She beckoned to them, urging them closer, and they pushed out of their row and raced down the aisle and sat on the floor, right below the stage, directly in front of the mayor.

"Isn't this the loveliest thing!" Chelsie called softly. "Isn't it just brilliant! Hi, Nichelle. Are you still shaky?"

"Promise you won't move!" Nichelle said. "No matter what anyone says, DO NOT LEAVE THAT SPOT! We absolutely, completely need you right there!"

"Look, Nichelle!" Barbie said from behind her.

Nichelle turned.

"Over in the corner, leaning against the wall. Do you see him?"

Nichelle followed Barbie's pointed finger. Ed Brook was standing there, watching them and grinning happily. When he saw that she noticed him, he raised his hand and waved. Nichelle waved back. Then she turned and looked at Barbie.

"Did you tell him?" Nichelle asked.

Barbie nodded. "I wanted to surprise you," she said. "And I knew he'd want to come."

Suddenly, as if by magic, the room grew still. Everyone, even the students, stopped talking and a terrifying hush fell over the room.

Nichelle's body tightened. She opened her mouth to speak, but she could not think of anything at all to say. For the first time in her life, her mind went blank.

And then something miraculous happened. She felt just fine. She could do this. No problem at all.

"Welcome, everyone," she announced. "We're here to tell you about the African Burial Ground and our recent discovery. It all began with a man named Ed Brook. Mr. Brook, would you raise your hand?"

Ed Brook stepped forward and waved to the crowd.

"Mr. Brook owns a small brownstone on the edge of the African Burial Ground."

Nichelle turned and nodded toward Barbie.

Barbie was ready. She flicked on the television and ran the video that she had shot. The tape was perfect, and the editing flawless, and when Barbie paused the projector the audience clapped.

They showed the slides and the interview with Ed Brook, and then Nichelle continued the mystery and introduced the evidence.

When Nichelle's clear, vivid photographs of the bone and the vase flashed on the screen, the audience cheered. Tori and Ana let out loud two-finger whistles that shook the room and left everyone laughing. Nichelle had kept the tension building, and when the surprise came, they applauded her.

The crowd was still applauding when Nichelle noticed the big man standing by the back door. She leaned over and poked Barbie.

"Look," she whispered. "In the back of the room. Do you see who I see?"

Nichelle wondered when Mr. Curtis had entered. She tried to decipher the expression on his face and his body language, but it was impossible from this distance.

They had been careful not to mention his name, but the sign with "Curtis Compound" had been clearly visible in Barbie's film. She wondered how he felt about it all. She had to assume that he wasn't pleased.

They had stopped the construction of his building, after all. And he had lost a lot of money.

As the applause died down, Curtis shook his head, turned, and left the auditorium. For just a second Nichelle felt sorry for him.

When he was gone, Nichelle sat silently for a moment, thinking about what they had done. Then she stood and joined Barbie at the front of the stage.

"Thank you for coming," she said in a strong confident voice. "We hope you'll all pay a visit to the burial ground, and please, please respect the history of all the members of this great city."

When they were finished, Nichelle and Barbie jumped off the stage and joined Mrs. Watson, the mayor, and Lara, Ana, Chelsie, and Tori. Ed Brook came over and thanked them all, and then he left, smiling. His brownstone was safe — a true historical site now.

"Well, young ladies," Mr. Budge said, joining them. "That will earn you a very nice extra-credit grade. I'm sure you'll be pleased."

Nichelle and Barbie thanked him and sat down in the front row. Nichelle felt overwhelmingly wonderful. Tonight she would sleep and tomorrow she and Barbie would write the article for the newspaper. Tori would help them post their information on the website, and that would be that.

A pang of sadness passed over her. She would be sorry to see it all end.

One by one her friends passed by and gave her a hug. They were all special, each in her own way. Lara, artistic and generous. Ana, straightforward and athletic. Chelsie, poetic and kind. Tori, exciting and fun. And Barbie, of course. Barbie was so trusting and enthusiastic. She loved them all.

"By the way, Nichelle," her mother said when everyone was gone and they were alone, "these were delivered to the house this morning right after you left. I think they're your proofs."

Nichelle's heart began to beat hard again. The envelope was from *Teen Style*.

She took the envelope aside and opened it alone, glancing through the pictures quickly, one at a time, then studying them more slowly. There she was in a bathing suit, in shorts, in the little dress.

She liked the way she looked. Yes, she looked just fine.

"Well?" her mother called from behind her. "How are they?"

Nichelle turned and shrugged. She wasn't sure what to say about them, so she just handed the envelope to her grandmother and waited as M'dear, smiling proudly, flipped through them.

"I think they're wonderful," Mrs. Watson said. "I think they're just beautiful. You are on a roll, Nichelle Watson. You are definitely on a roll."

Yes, thought Nichelle. *I'm on a roll. A great wild wonderful roll.*

That night, Nichelle was in bed by eight o'clock and asleep by 8:05. Her dreams were perfect.

Dear Niecy,

Hey girl, thanks for writing me back so fast. I knew you'd forgive your cuz.

So much stuff has happened since I wrote you the last time, I don't even know where to begin. I'm on my way to a modeling gig, so I can't make this long. But for now I'll just say I've been learning a lot about who I am and what I can do in this world, and girl, it's a lot.

And thanks for inviting me to New Orleans. I'd love to come. Just have to figure out how and when, clear it with the folks, and I'm there. Either that or how about you come up here? New York is the flip side of N'Orleans, cool! We're so lucky to live in the two coolest cities in the USA!

XOXOXO,
Nichelle

GENERATI✱N BEAT

I.H. STUDENTS UNEARTH A PIECE OF HISTORY AND SAVE SACRED BURIAL GROUND

At a press conference on Friday morning, two I.H. students presented a spectacular multi-media presentation that showed how a vital piece of New York history almost vanished under tons of concrete. Nichelle Watson and Barbie Roberts showed a video and slides and spoke of their incredible fight to save the African Burial Ground in lower Manhattan from being the site of yet another of Bruce Curtis's mammoth office buildings.

The two brave students described a race against time to find proof that the burial ground actually did date from the 18th century. The girls dug in the backyard of Ed Brook, who lives next to the burial ground.

This dig produced an amazing find: a bone! Tests conducted at the office of Grace Watson, Nichelle's mother and a New York City historical preservationist, showed that the bone, from the skeleton of a dog, did in fact date from the 1700s.

The results of this finding led the Mayor to halt construction of Mr. Curtis's new building. Because of the importance of this historical site, no further development will be done on this land. The site of the African Burial Ground is safe, thanks to Nichelle and Barbie, two of I.H.'s finest.

SUMMARY INFORMATION

Whether you are writing a school report or writing an article for your newspaper, one of the best tools you can use is the Internet. Schools across the country are going online, most public libraries have internet access, and many homes have computers. If you are able to use a computer to do research, you will be able to learn about anything in the world by following a few simple steps.

BE SMART ABOUT USING
THE INTERNET

First, ask your parents to install software that will filter out any adult material. Because the internet is used by adults and children, there is some information available that you don't want to see. Also, talk about the internet with your parents so you can set up rules about when you can use the computer.

USE A SEARCH ENGINE

Anything you want to learn about will be listed on one of the major search engines. Click search on the toolbar on your screen, and when the engine appears, type in the topic you are researching. You 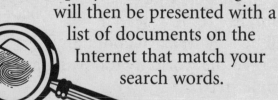 will then be presented with a list of documents on the Internet that match your search words.

FOLLOW LINKS

The first website you visit may not be exactly what you are looking for, but if it is close, look for the suggested links. If one of these looks close to your topic, click on it.

BOOKMARK YOUR FAVORITE SPOTS

Every online service describes this differently, but they all offer a way to mark a website that you want to remember: bookmark, "favorites," or "hot." This will save time in the future.

PRINT AS YOU GO

As always, keep a file of important information. Having copies of the information will save time when you actually start writing.

DON'T MISS **GENERATI✱N GIRL** #7:
STAGE FRIGHT

Barbie is thrilled with her new acting break —
a leading role in a local children's theater produc-
tion. There are rumors that the theater is haunted,
but Barbie knows there's no such thing as ghosts.
Can all of the scary things that happen to the pro-
duction be just a strange coincidence? Barbie is
determined to get to the bottom of the mystery.

CHECK OUT **generationgirl.com**
FOR MORE INFORMATION ON THE
GENERATION GIRLS!